BLAND SHIRE LIBRARY

 Y0-BZZ-591

Ruby's Potty

Paul and Emma Rogers

little ORCHARD

For Ruby - who else!

ORCHARD BOOKS
96 Leonard Street, London EC2A 4XD
Orchard Books Australia
Unit 31/56 O'Riordan Street, Alexandria, NSW 2015
ISBN 1 84121 664 X (hardback)
ISBN 1 84121 102 8 (paperback)
First published in Great Britain in 2001
First paperback publication in 2002
Text © Paul Rogers 2001
Illustrations © Emma Rogers 2001
The rights of Paul Rogers to be identified as the author and
Emma Rogers to be identified as the illustrator of this work have been
asserted by them in accordance with the
Copyright, Designs and Patents Act, 1988.
A CIP catalogue record for this book is available from the British Library.
1 3 5 7 9 10 8 6 4 2 (hardback)
1 3 5 7 9 10 8 6 4 2 (paperback)
Printed in Singapore

Ruby's got a potty.

She rides it round the floor.

The trouble is, she doesn't know
Just what a potty's for.

BLAND SHIRE LIBRARY

She hides it . . .

She slides it . . .

She puts it
on her head.

And when it's nearly
night time,

She makes it rabbit's bed.

She takes it to
the playground.

She takes it to the park.

She fills it up with animals -

Just like Noah's Ark.

It's handy in
the sandpit.

For carrying
things, it's great.

But when it's really needed —

Where is it?

Oops!

Too late.

"No nappy on," says Ruby.
"No nappy any more."

(But still she doesn't really know,
Just what a potty's for.)

BLAND SHIRE LIBRARY

She stays on it for ages.

Then, "Look!" calls Ruby, "Look!"

But all she's showing Daddy,
Is something in her book.

She sits her teddies one by one,

All round it in a ring.

If Mummy sits *her*
on it though,

She never
does a thing!

She puts it in her trolley,

And pushes
it around.

But when it's time for dinner,

She's nowhere to be found.

BLAND SHIRE LIBRARY

She isn't in the playhouse,

Or underneath the tree.

Whatever is she doing?

Wherever can she be?

Then, "Come and look!" calls Ruby,

With potty at the door.

Hooray!

Now Ruby really knows
Just what a potty's for!

BLAND SHIRE LIBRARY